Here's to You, America!

 LITTLE SIMON

An imprint of Simon & Schuster Children's Publishing Division

1230 Avenue of the Americas, New York, New York 10020

Manufactured in the United States of America

10 9 8 7 6 5 4 3 2

ISBN 0-689-85163-4

Adapted from the works of Charles M. Schulz

Here's to You, America!

By Charles M. Schulz
Adapted by Justine and Ron Fontes
Cover art adapted by Paige Braddock
Interior art adapted by Peter and Nick LoBianco
Based on the television episode "The Birth of the Constitution"
from the miniseries *This Is America, Charlie Brown*
produced by Lee Mendelson and Bill Melendez

LITTLE SIMON

New York   London   Toronto   Sydney   Singapore

Good grief! In 1787 America was a mess! Winning the Revolutionary War was hard enough. Now the thirteen states were taking their first steps toward becoming a united nation. They had to decide on a government—or risk turning into a lawless land where no one would be safe.

On May 25, everyone was busy, especially the Peanuts gang. On top of their usual chores, Charlie Brown and his friends had to clean up Independence Hall in Philadelphia, where a secret meeting was being held to create the new government.

Linus ran through the door of Charlie Brown's cabin. "Come on! We're late!"

"All right, everybody, here are our jobs for the convention," Linus announced. "Marcie and Peppermint Patty will be in charge of bringing water to the delegates."

"What's a delegate?" asked Peppermint Patty.

"A delegate is a representative. This convention will have several delegates from each state," Linus explained. Then he turned to Snoopy.

"You be the watchdog. This secret convention is not open to the public. Only fifty-five delegates will be here."

Linus continued. "Lucy, you need to mop the floor. Sally, your job is to see that all the inkwells are kept full."

Sally winked at Linus. "Whatever you say, Sweet Baboo!"

"What about me?" Charlie Brown asked. "What's my job?"

"You can be in charge of valet parking," Linus said.

Just then a big white horse trotted up. Charlie Brown took the reins and looked up at the tall man striding confidently toward the convention hall.

"That's General George Washington," Linus said. "He's going to lead the convention."

Charlie Brown felt proud even to be near the hero's horse! Without the brave and brilliant general, America might never have won its freedom from England.

Unfortunately, Snoopy didn't recognize General Washington.
He growled fiercely and blocked the door.
"No! Snoopy, no! Let him in!" Linus yelled.

"What's this convention all about?" Charlie Brown asked Linus.
Linus explained that since winning its independence, America had been a loose collection of thirteen states. To become a great country, the states would have to unite under one central government.

"The trouble is that some states want different things," Linus said. "Some people think the central government should be powerful. Others think the states should be left to rule themselves."

The convention began with a discussion about dividing the government into different parts called "branches." One branch, the Legislative, would make the laws. Another branch, the Judicial, would enforce the laws. A third branch, the Executive, would oversee it all.

But how would ordinary citizens participate in the Legislative branch?

Roger Sherman from Connecticut thought the people should be kept out of the government as much as possible. James Madison of Virginia disagreed. He felt that the people had to vote for at least one branch, or it wouldn't be a free government at all!

Linus agreed with Madison: Like a good climbing tree, the American government needed at least one branch close enough to the ground for ordinary citizens to reach with their votes.

As the argument heated up, the morning sun beat through the windows and turned the hall into a furnace! Linus's head started to spin. What was fair? What was right? Which system would help preserve justice and freedom?

Linus suddenly realized he was very thirsty! He figured the delegates must be thirsty too.

Linus poked his head outside to call for water. Peppermint Patty and Marcie were ready—at least they thought they were. The girls reached for their pails. "Hey! They're empty!" Peppermint Patty exclaimed.

Peppermint Patty and Marcie hurried back to the well to refill their pails. Then they raced back to the convention hall. Building a democracy was thirsty work!

After many days, the delegates finally decided that there should be two parts of the Legislative branch: the House of Representatives and the Senate. The people should vote for the House of Representatives, and the number of members would be determined according to the population of each state.

But the second half, the Senate, would be different. Members would be elected by state assemblies. And there would be an equal number of senators for each state, no matter how big or small the state was.

Some delegates thought the House and Senate needed to be balanced by a single leader—a president—who would head the Executive branch.

"I think it should be a queen," Lucy declared. "A beautiful queen!"

They struggled to decide what kind of leader
a free country needed and how that leader should
be chosen. Many voices shouted at once.
George Washington pounded his gavel.

Linus was worried. "They can't seem to agree
on anything."

"I think we are in big trouble, sir," Marcie added.

"What does it all mean?" Peppermint Patty
asked.

Linus shrugged. "If they can't work out
a compromise, the whole convention may fail.
Without laws to protect people and property
and a system to enforce the laws, our country
will be a mess!"

The arguments went on through the hot Philadelphia summer. Day after humid day, week after steamy week, the Peanuts gang witnessed the nation's slow struggle to create its own government. Sally tiptoed between the shouting delegates to fill their inkwells.

All the delegates cared very deeply about government: But did they care enough to compromise and reach an agreement?

The Peanuts gang was tired and worried.

"We've been working at this convention for almost two months," Peppermint Patty said. She had walked to the water well too many times to count!

"Do you think everything is going to fail, Linus?" Marcie asked.

Linus sighed. "I hear that every day some of the delegates threaten to quit and go home. No one seems to know what's going to happen."

Lucy shook her head. "If they would just elect a beautiful queen, that would solve everything."

But for a long time nothing was solved. It seemed as if the Peanuts gang would spend the rest of their lives cleaning the convention hall and listening to debates. Three months felt like thirty!

The delegates had finally agreed that one leader would be elected—the president—not two or three leaders, and not a king or queen. Now they had to work on the Judicial branch.

Charlie Brown hoped the delegates would stop at three branches. If they tried for a whole tree, this convention would never end!

Charlie Brown got his wish. The delegates settled on three branches of government. And on September 17, almost four long months after the convention began, they signed a document explaining how those branches would balance each other out. It was called the Constitution. "At least we don't have to carry any more buckets!" Peppermint Patty said.

Everyone seemed very happy, but Charlie Brown was still confused! That night he asked Linus, "What does all this mean?"

Linus took out a roll of paper. "Well, let me read you what they wrote, Charlie Brown," he said.

"'We the People of the United States, in Order to form a more perfect Union, establish Justice, insure domestic Tranquility, provide for the common defence, promote the general Welfare, and secure the Blessings of Liberty to ourselves and our Posterity, do ordain and establish this Constitution for the United States of America.'"

Linus smiled. "And that's what freedom is all about, Charlie Brown!"

Peppermint Patty said, "I bet those delegates are glad to finally go home!"

Linus sighed. "The trouble is, their work has only begun. In order to make it the law of the land, the delegates must get nine out of thirteen states to approve the Constitution. That may take months, even years—or it may never happen."

"Government doesn't seem to be an easy business," Charlie Brown observed.
Linus agreed. "Freedom isn't a very easy business either, Charlie Brown."
But finally, on June 21, 1788, New Hampshire cast the deciding vote to approve the
Constitution! The United States had become truly united—and the best was yet to come.

In the years that followed, the Constitution helped to keep the American government just as the nation's founders intended—and to make America a land of freedom and justice for all!